HENRY NEILSEN

Eleanor's Mind

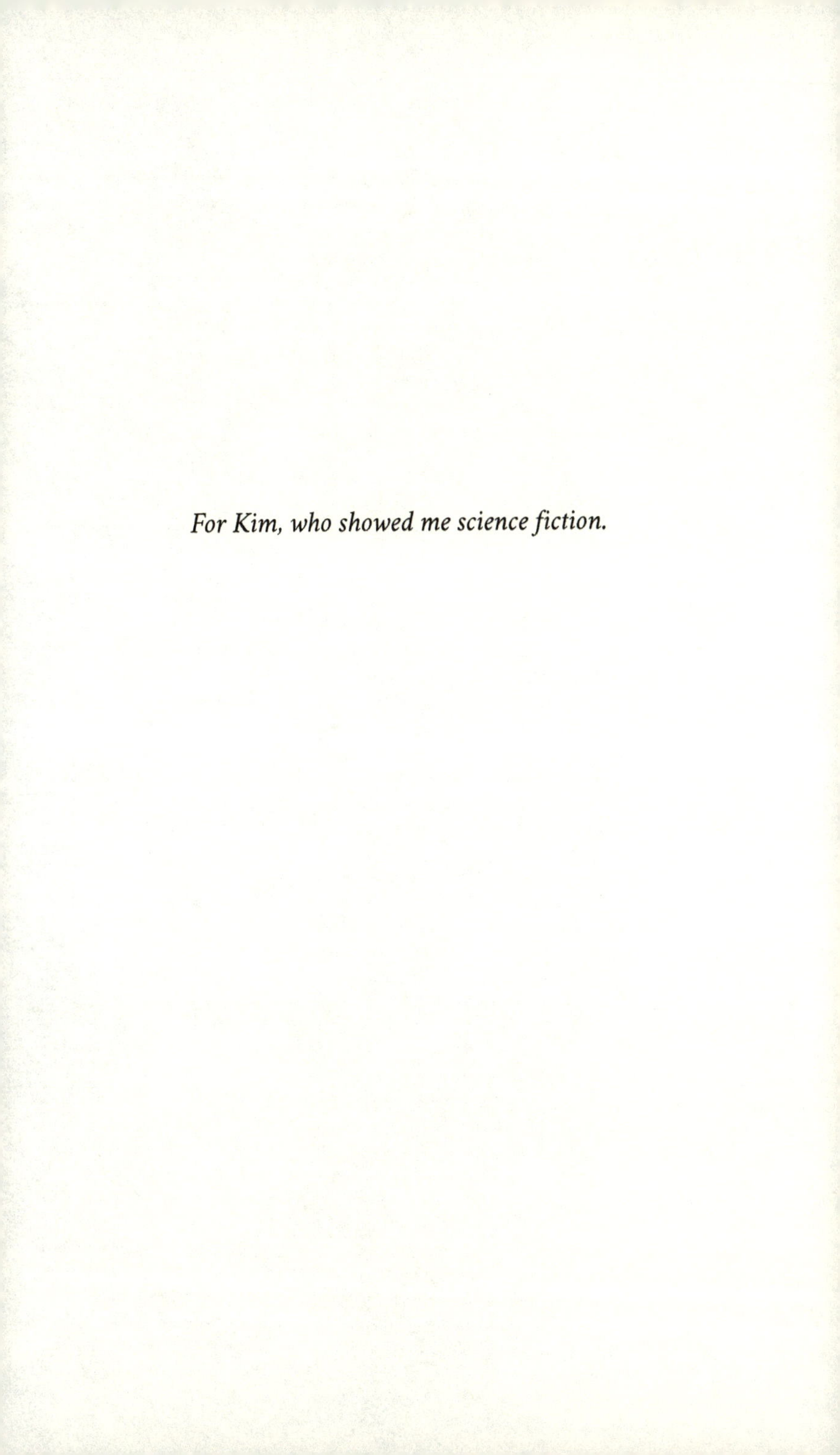

For Kim, who showed me science fiction.

Eleanor's Mind

The voice, when it came through what she assumed must be a speaker, held the cracks of a man at the edge of a long run of very little sleep. The whole sound spoke of a deep, tired sigh.

"Um, Eleanor?" the hesitation was tangible. She looked up.

"How are you feeling?" it said.

She considered the question as she looked around. She didn't know where she was, and when she tried to think of what she'd done to get herself there a deep ache slipped through her entire consciousness. She was in the center of a uniformly lit room, unfurnished and unadorned, except for what seemed to be a floor lamp left curiously unplugged. She noticed too that the room had no doors or windows, and her confused calm gave way to a gnawing uneasiness.

She spun, searching for the voice's origin, looking for speaker grills, light fittings, fire sprinklers or any of the other fixtures to be expected in what seemed like a typical room. There was none of it. The room formed a perfect cube, in which light seemingly emanated from each atom in the stale air, and cast a perfect, reflectionless opacity on the walls themselves. She went to rub her eyes, hoping that the uncanny nature of her experience required nothing more than the blinking away of sleep.

She had no hands.

She had no arms, either. As a matter of fact, as she cast her eyes around, she saw no part of her own body interrupting her view of the space. As she spun she found that she had no physical limits, no inhibitions of her regular body. Eleanor panicked, and tried to call out, but found that she had no mouth to call from. Adrenaline spiked through her mind, and she stared helplessly at the void. *Help!* She tried to scream. The room responded with growing blackness, followed closely by the loss of her consciousness.

* * *

"I *told* you, she needs a body!" the tech shouted through the tumult, shoving his glasses up the crest of his nose. Around him, the rest of his team dashed between workstations, reading the patterns of Eleanor's brain activity. The tale was written in the numbers; these waveforms belonged to a person exhibiting a state of extreme anxiety. "You can't just make a digital copy of a person's brain, stick them in a void, and assume they'll be fine. They need stimulus!" the tech snapped to someone behind him, then turned to the other workers. "Shut her off! We need to handle this before any mental degradation sets in."

The source material was dangerously close to losing its integrity, and damage caused by the simulacrum had proven to be irreversible. The lab couldn't afford to lose this data.

The woman standing behind the tech watched coolly from the corner, the concern in her eyes masked by the poor lighting on the outside of the bullpen and years of experience. She eyed the lead technician, whose uniform hung dishevelled over his small frame. He had turned to hunch over his keyboard, raking his glasses up his nose once more.

The woman turned up her chin, gesturing to the screen. "I thought you said the *time* problem would be the last delay."

"I expected no more *major* delays, is what I said." he clarified, "This is our first run-through, remember?" The brain-in-a-box experiment was one that should have been more thoroughly beta tested, or even alpha tested, before being used on a critical subject. It was just that this particular woman's health insurance policy had had enough to cover her for experimental procedures. Besides, between the accident and this procedure, she was likely to end up brain dead anyway, so why not? It's not like she could be expected to survive being sideswiped by a bus at that speed.

The time problem had been a difficult one. As it had turned out, you couldn't just *upload* a consciousness to a computer and expect it to communicate with you. The human consciousness was a simulation strung across finite state machines, each of which deconstructed into a highly complex version of a throughput device; receive signals, pass them on. The knowledge of how 'time' passed, and therefore its ability to *process* thought, relied on a function five steps down the line knowing how long it had been since the previous steps had taken place. In a human, this was handled by a series of extremely large neurons that enveloped the brain. These acted as a relay system to the claustrum, which linked the centres of the brain together in such a way that allowed consciousness. Unfortunately, a supercomputer, for all its advantages, still boiled down to digital technology that had no such neural interconnectedness. The result was that the technical team had essentially withdrawn the entirety of Eleanor as a static memory, no more capable of independent thought than a calculator, videogame, or spreadsheet. The concern had been that if she were to continue to function as a conscious being, there must be some constant, continued processing of information while in the computer. That way, they would be able to ensure her "mind" stayed active until her mangled body could be returned to a state fit for human habitation.

His team was intelligent, and capable. It had only taken them four nights of round-the-clock shifts to fabricate and code a working awareness of time and entropy into the woman's digitised brain. An electronic neuron that talked to the memory bank made it all work. At least, it *had* worked. Now they had another problem.

The woman gestured sharply to the lead technician, beckoning him. "Explain to me what you just said," she said. The others in the room continued to work on the simulation of the woman's mind, bringing it into stasis as he gathered his thoughts.

The lead technician, Laurence, heaved a ragged sigh and peered through his thick rims. He knew that this was going to be a large part of the coming weeks. The risk and expense the company had taken on in trying to save Eleanor was immense, and it was the sole responsibility of this woman to ensure its success. A heady task, and he didn't envy her. Still, he didn't want to have to tell her all the theory behind the enormous cognitive sandbox they were building, especially as he didn't fully understand it himself yet. "At the moment we've got her conscious, and we've given her the perception of having heard something in a room, and a room to hear it in. But that's not how the real world works," he grumbled, shaking his head. "We aren't *brains* in *rooms*, we're brains in *bodies* in rooms. By taking away the part of her that actually connects her processing plant to her sense organs, we're throwing her for a loop. She can't process where the interface is happening."

"So, what do we do about that?" The woman asked.

* * *

"Eleanor," the voice came again. Firmer this time, less tired.

Eleanor's last memory had been of panicking, she recalled, although she couldn't remember why. The room was still in the eerie state of self-illumination that it was before, and the silence was complete. Even her movements made no noise as she walked. She looked down. Her hands and arms were slick and flawless. It reminded her of the look of a new gadget after you peeled of the protective layer of plastic. Her clothing hung stiff from her body, swaying unnaturally, and her legs were slightly askew from where her mind told her they should be. As she watched, they shifted, sliding slowly to align with her expectations. Eleanor looked up to stare ahead instead, eyes wide. Her mind must have been playing tricks on her.

What the hell is going on? she uttered, although no words came with the thought. The voice seemed to understand her, though.

"You were in a collision," it said, and as the words rolled silently through her she was brought back to the night it happened. Eleanor had been at work late, catching up on yet another day of intense consultation sessions with the lawyers about some merger or other. She'd been rolling in to her third week of fourteen-hour days, and she was exhausted. All it had taken on the drive home was a short lapse in concentration. There had been a flash of light, the sound of breaking glass, and the snap of her body to the left, before everything had gone black. She'd woken up here, in this room.

Why can't I speak? she asked.

"We're working on that." The voice replied. "It seems as though your mind doesn't like the idea of being dissociated from your body, so we're building it. In the interest of expediency, you have the bare essentials, and we'll add functionality as we go."

Where is my real body?

"As soon as we can get an image through to you, we will. Your body is in the intensive care unit of the Mercy Hospital downtown. You were in… pretty bad shape when you arrived."

The voice went on to explain that at present she was in a simulation, and that there had been a chance of her going brain dead after the accident. Rather than allowing that to happen, they had taken the drastic step of porting her into the computer. Eleanor listened and understood that the course of action chosen by the doctors had been the best of a bad situation. This technology was still being tested, and so there were no guarantees, but at least they were trying to save her conscious mind. That gratified her a bit.

As Eleanor was listening, what she now understood as her 'eyes' began to wander around the room. Its perfection was unsettling, as was the curious illumination that emanated from everywhere and nowhere. It was the visual equivalent of silence, she realised. The visual part of her brain telling her of the absolute nothingness there was to see.

Spots of colour in the room began to shift curiously. Small mirages danced across her vision, appearing and disappearing of their own accord, and flying in and out of the walls. Some of them began to sing; a guttural rumble from a silver ribbon that flew from the left wall, a high-pitched keening from a kite-like structure in front of her, burbling and jumping and disappearing like a cacophonous orchestra.

The voice had stopped, and the mirages grew larger. Louder. More insistent. They swept in on her, threatening to smother her. She knew that she couldn't technically be breathing, but claustrophobia left her feeling breathless all the same. She tried to shout out but couldn't, and the shapes roared and careened in their chaotic motion.

* * *

"What do you mean she's *hallucinating?*" Laurence demanded. The realisation that at some level, Eleanor was going to need a body to interact with, had meant that he could hand over the simulation to the 3D environment technicians, and he'd had a blissful fourteen hours of sleep in one of the cots at the research centre. Still, the dawning realisation that these kinds of high priority bug fixes were going to be a mainstay of the project was a hard pill to swallow. His job had grown exponentially in scope from 'manage an enormous memory bank' to 'keep a young woman from dying' a little too quickly. It left him strained. "This time last week we couldn't get her to fucking *think,* and now she's *making shit up on her own?*" His appreciation of the complexities of human consciousness, already quite profound, had been forced to expand over the last few days. There was still so much about this process that none of them really understood. *Too much,* he thought, as he walked back around to the monitoring station.

"She's freaking out because her environment is too perfect, yet not as responsive as it should be by now," a young tech responded, the frustration eking out of the corners of his voice.

"Her mind is trapped in a room that gives her almost no sensory feedback, and our brains aren't built for a dearth of stimulus like that. She needs something to make her brain switch on."

"Right, well, we're trying to fix that, but the Environments guys take time." Laurence removed his glasses to massage his brow, replacing them before continuing. "What's likely to happen here if we leave it? Like, what if we just leave her to hallucinate until we can make the environment more real?" The idea of leaving the test subject to hallucinate vividly didn't sit well with him. Eleanor *was* a human being, whether or not she had a body to match right now. Induced schizophrenia seemed cruel, even if there was no other option.

"At a guess, the hallucinations will impede her ability to process information. In the first instance, they'll continue to do what they're doing now." The younger tech gestured to a screen before him. Printed on it were erratic brainwaves, scrabbling across the axes of the graph. "But I suspect that the continued lack of 'real' stimulus will cause an amplifying effect on the hallucinations the longer we allow them to run. There have been tests done on sensory deprivation in the real world in the past. The results were never good."

"So we need to fill her up with distractions, or she'll keep making her own?" Laurence asked, scratching his chin. "and eventually, we're looking at a sort of… synthesized schizophrenia?"

"Essentially, but probably more acute." the young tech said.

Laurence sighed, eyes tracing the brainwaves as they danced. He finally turned to eye the young man. "How long does she have?"

They gazed at the screen together. Eleanor's brain activity was already showing significant signs of distress, and probably wouldn't last another day or two. The environments team was working at their fastest, but they wouldn't be able to get a full suite of sensory assets built in time. Over the next two hours, Laurence and the young tech discussed the highest priority items. They were going to send a basic set of assets to the environments team as a stop gap, when the project director walked in.

"Is there a problem?" she asked, surveying the two men and placing her coffee on a nearby desk. Laurence and his tech stiffened to the voice, turning slowly to face it while trying to control the urge to roll their eyes. The counter was filled with sketches and stationery. A brief outline of sensory input data sat inset in the computer's window before them, displaying the rapidly deteriorating brain activity of Eleanor.

Laurence quickly outlined the predicament. The director listened, leaning on the desk where her coffee began to cooled, forgotten.

"How long do we have?" she asked.

"With the level of brain activity we're seeing here? And the level of distress?" Laurence asked, and the director's flat, curt expression forced him quickly onwards. "I think if we take longer than six hours, our potential disaster case becomes exponentially more likely." he said, then added: "At a best guess."

The director nodded and surveyed the terminal which displayed Eleanor's brain function. The morning sun shone through the triple glazing, falling softly on her right side as she regarded the complex series. She glanced over at the environment screen, where a 3D model of a white room shifted back and forth. A point in its centre defined where Eleanor thought she was, and a crude model of her body was inset in a separate window. The body was cowering, hands flailing in the air. The director looked up.

"So, we need something to occupy her senses that will give enough data to be able to stimulate her brain…" the director pondered. "That doesn't have to be 3D assets right? We can do it with other sensory data?"

Laurence considered, and nodded. "No, it doesn't have to be visual I suppose. Just something that will give her senses something to work with."

"What about white noise?"

* * *

Eleanor held on to herself in a desperate embrace, one that in any caring universe she could have shared with someone else. The glitched creatures careened and cavorted around her, and their noise was deafening. The voice that had let her know where she was had long since been unable to cut through the roar of the shifting mass. The creatures themselves had not held on to their individual forms. They flew into and out of each other, morphing and swirling, threatening and oppressing. She cried silent, tearless sobs as the world around her grew smaller and louder. Eleanor closed her eyes, but the creatures were still there. Squeezing her eyes shut and running to a corner, Eleanor tried to vanish into it. To disappear. To make it all just stop. She quietly realised that she was losing her mind, when suddenly the unending shrieking receded. In its place, she could hear nothing but the soft hiss of an old AM radio, untuned.

The creatures fled from the darkness of her closed eyes. She didn't believe they'd gone and so she was still silently holding on to herself, leaning against the false wall. *I have no way to protect myself here*, she thought, and wept silently again, staring into the corner. As she slipped into a dreamlike trance, staring at the wall, the soft hiss continued. Her mind felt free again, but the quiet terror of being trapped would not recede.

* * *

"She doesn't sleep." The director noted.

"Does she have to?" Laurence asked, closing a file on his screen in a quietly guilty movement. The director didn't seem to notice.

"I don't know." the younger tech responded quickly. "We know sleep is an important process to recover the mind from the build-up of toxicity that gets acquired over the course of a normal day. But she doesn't have those chemical reactions happening," he said, "What's more, we can't see any data suggesting that there is an equivalent of that toxicity build-up happening. She's just a five and a half petabyte file of data in constant flux. She doesn't seem as concerned by the lack of sleep as she was about the lack of sensory input though, so I'm happy enough to leave it as is, if she is." The young man gulped, then added: "And if both of you think it's a good idea, I guess."

"I'll ask her." Laurence said, "We're pretty close to giving her a look at herself in the ward. They say her brain activity has slowed substantially, but they think once the capillaries are repaired they can reinstate her into her original brain stem with no harm."

"That's good to hear. The timeline seems to be working out well." The director looked at her watch. "And with that, I'm going home. Let me know if anything comes up."

"Will do," Laurence hummed, waving her off. "Thanks."

"You may as well go, too." he said to the younger technician, who needed no further prompting. He packed his things and began to head out the door.

Once he heard the door click, Laurence opened the computer window up again. On it was a crudely drawn wireframe of a human skeleton, with nodes representing joints. Over the course of several hours, the armature was constructed, with musculature, skin, hair and other features. At some point Laurence stopped tinkering at the keyboard. He backed up his work, leaned backward, and stared at the screen depicting Eleanor's room. His eyes were tired, but intently focused as he watched Eleanor pace carefully around.

* * *

The room was different now, Eleanor noticed. Where before there had been a uniform and constant glow, casting no shadows - yet somehow still allowing the edges of the room to form their shape - now it seemed as though the 'ceiling', for what it was worth, was the source of the light. The corners at the bottom of the room were more softly lit in comparison, and the light had a warmth to it that hadn't been there before. She wondered when that had happened. The auditory hiss that had stopped her overwhelming hallucinations had long ceased to be of notice to her, and now her major issue was how to occupy her time. A constant, gnawing fear had given way to boredom.

"What can we get you?" the voice asked. It was the same voice every time. The team of scientists and technicians working on her must have decided that listening to a consistent, unchanging voice would help her feel a connection to another human being in some way. They were right.

Eleanor considered the question. She'd always been someone

to get work done indoors, with the outdoors reserved for leisure, exploring the little creeks and gullies about an hour's drive from the city. She hadn't ever been one for recreational reading or watching news feeds or browsing the internet. Being stuck in a well-lit cube frustrated her.

"I'd like to do something that occupies my body, if possible." she said at last, "If not, can I get a screen that I can at least read something on? Or the news? I'd like to know what's going on in the world." She had no real way of telling how long she'd even *been* in the room. The voice had told her they'd had to 'switch her off' a couple of times. The thought of being turned on and off like some kind of household appliance concerned her.

The light was constant and confused her circadian rhythm, so she never felt tired. Logically she knew how strange that was, but the feeling associated with the completion of a task and its related lethargy simply didn't come into her consciousness.

"We'll see what we can do on the news front." the voice said, "we can probably put something in like a set of gym equipment. It obviously won't affect the composition of your body in the real world, but it may assist in providing something akin to the dopamine hit of actually working out."

"Sure," Eleanor shrugged. *At least it's something other than waiting to see if I can get back into my real body.* She had been assured some time ago that she'd be able to see her body. Apparently, there had been a bleed into her brain which had been concerned would render her braindead, but the surgical team had swooped in and cleaned up whatever it was that needed cleaning from her skull cavity. She didn't know. All she knew was that now her body was an empty vessel, and the physical manifestation of herself was not in any real sense her anymore.

It was an uncomfortable thought.

* * *

"Exercise equipment," the director said incredulously.

"It makes sense. It seems she was a fairly active person before, so it's not a crazy request. It's just that in terms of physical returns, there's not really any point for her to do it." Laurence said.

"What's the issue with it then?" the director asked.

"We need to get the environments team to alter her body at the same time as when they introduce the equipment. And they can't turn her off; her brain patterns are fully stabilized and normal now, and I don't want to risk a reboot procedure again." They hadn't told Eleanor, as it would just worry her, but each time they started her up, there had been a spike in brain pattern which was so far unexplainable. Laurence thought it was most likely a boot-up procedure – some running of electricity through every node of the circuit that represented her brain. "She stays live until we transfer her back," he resolved, firmly.

"What's causing the spikes?" The director asked. She was leaning forward in her chair. Laurence knew as well as she did that her job was on the line. The decision to run this trial so soon had been reckless, and - if anyone started asking lawyer-type questions - probably illegal. Eleanor's entire consciousness *had* been relocated without her direct consent, after all.

"You know the old adage of 'we only use 10% of our brain'?" He asked.

"I know it's bullshit," The director replied.

"Exactly. It's like saying we only use one third of a traffic light. We use all of our brains, but the neural pathways are wired in such a way that only a part of it will be 'live' at any given time."

"Yes?"

"Well, every time we switch her back on, for some reason her consciousness does some sort of 'state check'. Floods the dataset with a heap of noise. I'm worried that if we do it too many times, a bunch of logic gates will switch, and we'll have an enormous file of useless static." *Not to mention we'd kill her,* he didn't add.

The director leaned back in her chair, rubbing her face. Eyeing her now, Laurence noticed how gaunt her face had become, and he must have looked similar. The dread of keeping someone *alive* in an environment they'd created, but didn't fully understand yet, was a terrifying concept. "Okay. Okay. So, we keep her running. What's the problem with the exercise gear again?" the director asked.

Laurence said, "Environments weren't concerned with how realistically her body behaved when they built it; they only needed her to think she had a logical location for her sensory data to be coming from. So Eleanor's cyber-body just obeys her commands, and doesn't have any logic about what she 'should' be capable of. If we put in a bunch of resistance equipment, she'll be able to just lift it. She'd be stronger than any bodybuilder and wouldn't feel the effects *at all.* Because her 'body' doesn't know that simulated matter is *supposed* to be heavy."

"Alright. Alright. I'll talk to environments." The director sighed. "Tell them to give her the sensation of weight, make a physics system that makes sense… and let them know it has to be a live upload that she can't notice." She hauled herself from her chair. "In the meantime, get a screen in there. Give her a documentary to watch, or something. Anything else?"

"We want to know when we can show her… you know. *Her.*" Laurence said. "She's asked a couple of times." He'd been speaking to her occasionally in the evening, outside the hours of work. He kept telling himself that he was just doing his professional duty by checking up on her.

The director sighed. "I'll talk to the team at Mercy. See if we can install some cameras in the room tomorrow."

* * *

The worst thing, Eleanor decided, was dealing with the passage of time. Now that her consciousness wasn't immediately in danger, her existence had become long, lonely, and quiet. Eleanor had found herself staring into space, her mind slipping into a quietly meditative state for what must have been hours at a time. She couldn't sleep, or eat, or drink to stave off the boredom, so she'd taken to yoga and stretching her shiny, too-perfect body over the floor of her cubicle. She'd realised the futility of holding on to frustration, and she was glad to hear that they had confidence in returning her to her body; being stuck in this room forever would be a special kind of hell.

The voice came and ripped her from her reverie. "Eleanor, do me a favour and close your eyes," it said, "we're about to import some assets and we aren't sure if you'll cope with their sudden existence in front of you, as it were."

Eleanor did so, and whatever part of her computerised mind the technicians had connected to her computerised body was disconnected from the feedback of the computerised environment. Everything went dark, and the blackness which took hold was too complete to be of reality. No hint of light sources behind eyelids. No sparkling or dancing artefacts on the retina. Just blackness. It was another jarring reminder of the unreality of the situation.

"Okay," the voice said, with the air of one handing out a present to a youngster on Christmas day, "open again".

The fact that they'd modelled it to look like a real-life video screen was funny to Eleanor, and she chuckled to herself. There it was, a remote control, and a little indicator LED on the side suggesting that the unit was in standby mode. There was a lounge in front of it in hospital-grade off-white, and the screen itself sat on a small stand. She smiled, and collapsed on the couch, reaching for the remote. At least there was *something* to do now.

"This is also the device we'll be using to send you updates from the hospital. We've spoken to the ICU team, and apparently you're through the worst of it. We'll be able to get a camera set up in your recovery room, though if there are any procedures you undergo, we'll not have you watch." the voice said.

Eleanor nodded. "Do we know how long that'll take?" She was concerned the extent of the crash's aftereffects. If it were bad enough that her entire consciousness was uploaded to a simulation, then it must have been a pretty terrible crash. What did she *look* like now? How bad were the physical effects on her body?

"Only a couple more hours. In the meantime, this screen has a link to a database of movies and shows you can watch. I think we got it from the server of one of our interns," the voice said, "hopefully it tides you over."

It certainly looked like the hard drive of a student, she mused a few hours later. Badly organised, idiosyncratic file naming and incomplete series of various shows, along with a frankly alarming amount of pornography. She browsed for a while, then settled on a procedural medical drama. It seemed appropriate for the situation.

* * *

"Are we sure this is a good idea?" The doctor asked the director. His dark eyes were glancing at the small camera setup in the corner. "She might panic. As you can see she's in bad shape, and the psychological effect of seeing yourself in a coma with this much… it's not a pretty picture."

"We can't hide her from it. She'll have to deal with it when she gets out, anyway." the director huffed, "And if we keep stalling, we're going to have her start worrying about what's happening to her. Our reassurance starts to seem like empty words if we refuse to show her what's going on."

The doctor grimaced. He knew that the director was right.

A call came through for the director as she nodded her assent. She slid a finger across the phone's screen, placing it to her ear. "Hi Laurence… okay. Yes, we're almost set up. Hold on, let me check and get back to you." She hung up and turned to the workers. "Are you nearly done?" She asked.

"Just about," a worker said, fiddling with something on the back of the camera, and checking against a small diagnostic tablet she'd brought with her. She turned to the doctor. "Nothing's in your way here, is it?" The doctor shook his head.

The worker had a final check of her diagnostics terminal. A series of green indicators flashed downward across the screen.

"We're good". She said.

* * *

Eleanor was on to the third season of her medical drama when she received contact from the voice again. She may have been imagining it, but he seemed uncomfortable. It was as though he'd been keeping a secret and it was about to be found out.

"We're about to give you access to your feed. You'll be able to see yourself for the first time since the accident. Be warned; you have sustained very serious injury, and that is apparent by sight alone. In addition, we are unsure of any potential psychological effects that may come from viewing yourself in a comatose and highly injured state." It paused, "Especially as we are unsure if your real body still has any brain function."

Eleanor considered, then said, "What are you concerned about? I'm just going to be looking at a picture of myself."

"You're going to be experiencing the first scientifically observable out-of-body experience that anyone in the world has ever had. You're going to be watching yourself in a state you know is unstable. You're probably frustrated that you're stuck in here. We don't think you're going to go crazy or anything, but we don't think it's unreasonable to expect that you might have some psychological trauma associated with it. People who are disfigured or seriously injured in accidents will often require counseling under normal circumstances, and this is anything but a normal circumstance."

He had a point, Eleanor admitted. She'd spent some time wondering how bad the accident must have been, but for some reason she'd never considered that there would be physical evidence, that her body might be just as corrupt as they were telling her that her brain was. The thought did make her uneasy, on reflection.

"Can I decide to turn it off?" she asked.

"Of course. Only say the word." There was genuine care there, she realised. He was worried about her.

"Okay," she said. Then, "Please show me."

* * *

"I hope this works," Laurence said.

The director eyed him knowingly. "You've double- and triple-checked everything. Let her see."

He sighed, then typed the command.

* * *

The medical drama dissolved from the AV set, and slowly changed to noise, then something else. An image coalesced and formed into a hospital room. An orderly was reading from a chart at the end of a bed, which housed a series of screens indicating vital signs and treatment schedules near its head. The walls were the particular cream colour that spoke of hospital-grade cleanliness the world over. Eleanor could practically smell the disinfectant.

The woman in the bed had her eyes closed, and was breathing shallowly, a quiet rasp coming every few seconds. The thick mop of curly auburn hair hung limp and greasy by her, tied into a messy bun by the orderlies. A gash ran from her left temple down to her neckline, and continued unseen under her shirt. It had been stitched up with exact precision, but the scar would still be ugly. And permanent. One of her arms and both her legs were in casts, and her remaining arm bore the pale memories of scabs that had grown out and away.

With a shock, Eleanor realised she was *looking at herself*. The recognition had taken longer than intended - she hadn't seen a real human body in such a long time that the initial connection to a human being had borne more weight than her own physical presence. She stared at the scar, massive and broken and ugly across one side of a face that was only beginning to show the signs of age. Her arms, usually corded with at least some musculature from a regular exercise regimen, were limp, thin and lifeless, a soft pall indicating their catabolic state. A blanket draped softly across her, hiding her view of her own self, and denying her of both the familiar and alien quality of her form.

"Eleanor." the voice came again.

"Yes?"

"Are you okay? This must be difficult..."

Eleanor didn't respond for a while. She found it almost impossible to get her eyes off the screen. *Not my real eyes,* she thought. *Those are shut, connected to a brain that isn't even working.* The woman, who she still didn't quite connect as herself, shuddered a little as a larger than usual rasp came from a breath. The cannula coming from her nostrils fogged in a steady rhythm.

"Eleanor?"

"Sorry. Yes. I'm okay. I just..." She hesitated. "You know that feeling... where you get a new haircut and you look at yourself and think 'surely I don't look like *that*'?"

The voice laughed gently. "Yes. It's always in the mirror when I get home," it said.

The thought of the disembodied voice taking a haircut was enough to bring Eleanor back from her reverie. She tore her eyes away from the screen, and turned to the corner of the room which she'd decided the voice emanated from - a curiosity that had slipped by her suddenly at the front of her mind.

"You know, you've been talking to me for God knows how long. I can't believe I've never asked if there's a reason it's always you talking to me?"

Again the voice laughed. "Yes, Eleanor. I'm the head of the technical team on this research project and it's my responsibility to get informed consent from you to everything that goes on while we're getting your body better. We use one point of contact because we thought it would be more disconcerting for you to have to speak to several different people and remember who was who."

Eleanor drifted back to her bed and sat cross legged on top of it. "Yeah, that's probably right. I don't think I'd like talking to too many people here. I think I appreciate the personal service, if I'm honest." she grinned.

"Absolutely. Plus, a single point of communication means that less chance of confusion when it comes to information gathering. Different interpretations can lead to people getting their wires crossed." the voice said.

"Yeah, we wouldn't want that," Eleanor agreed, then asked: "So, what's your name?"

"Laurence," the voice said.

"Call me Ellie. All my friends do."

* * *

Laurence sat silently for a moment. *This could be an issue.* He'd been warned against getting too close to the simulated version of the subject before they knew what the chances of success were. Losing a patient was always hard enough, but losing someone you had a rapport with when there was literally nothing you could do about it - that had to be even worse.

He glanced at his other screen, where the 3D model of the body he'd created was displayed. He should've deleted it by now, he knew that, but he continued not to. He had kept tinkering away, spending hours at the lab obsessing over tiny details. He'd been getting updates on Eleanor all the while, assessing her mental state through short conversations each evening.

The poor woman had been in there for weeks now and seeing herself on a slab with a bloody great scar across her body, and more plaster around her than a gyprock specialists house, must be at least a little traumatic. There couldn't be too much harm in keeping her company.

He leaned back toward the microphone. "Pleasure to meet you, Ellie."

Eleanor's voice answered back through the speaker; it might not actually sound like her, but it was a close enough approximation of a twenty something woman that it had become her voice to Laurence in the past weeks.

"I can't really imagine how bad it must have been to start with." the speaker rattled slightly as her voice transmitted through it. Audio quality had been the last thing on their minds when setting up the lab and it rendered the speakers sounding thin, tinny and underpowered. "What caused the scar? The big one on my face?"

How bad it must have been to start with, Laurence grimaced. He thought it best not to tell her how she'd looked when she'd come in for the first time, with shards of metal impaling her, blood and gore creating a shroud that made it nigh impossible to tell where the crash ended and the woman began. He shuddered slightly at the memory of it; he was a computer scientist, not a doctor or nurse, and his appetite for such things was not particularly high.

"Your face… It was a piece of glass from the windshield" he said, "the thing shattered, as it was supposed to, but the whole side of the windshield that attached to the A-pillar was caught in the plastic runnel that holds it. It scraped down your face and got lodged in your neck. It had to be removed surgically."

Eleanor's sensors registered a minor shock reaction. In the simulation's screen, she sat down on the couch again. "Holy shit."

"Yeah. you're lucky we got you in here in time. Your brain… it stopped functioning about three hours after we'd copied your consciousness. Extreme blunt trauma."

Her indicators were getting worse. Undue stress wasn't desirable, as they didn't know how much more her simulation would take before it started failing. "I can turn it off for you if you like? I understand it must be difficult." Laurence moved toward the monitor.

"No, it's okay," she said. "it's just… a lot." Her simulated body relaxed a bit, eyes still fixed on the screen. Laurence took a short second to admire the environment team's ability to accurately read intended body movements from her thoughts.

"Okay. I'm going to hand you personal control over it. You can watch yourself at any time. If we see too many stress markers, we'll let you know, but I think we can trust you to believe your own emotions, right?"

Eleanor smiled, and the mood monitor on one of the displays picked up. "Yeah," she said. "Of course."

"All good then."

"Laurence?"

"Yes, Ellie?"

"Where's my exercise equipment?"

* * *

Two days later the equipment came. Ellie had been sitting on her bed for a lot of it, looking up at the screen of herself. She realised she was in quite a unique situation, with the ability to watch her comatose body heal in real time - and to even be able to observe herself in this state at all. So, she watched with morbid curiosity as the orderlies came in and changed her bedpans, cleaned her wounds, idly gossiped in the way that workmates did, and generated their reports on her condition. The way the quiet solace of her room was broken only by the soft rasp of her breath, a rasp that grew fainter each day as she healed.

Eleanor sat cross-legged, hands in her lap with her mind staring emptily, as she tried to imagine what her face had looked like without the scar on it, when she was startled.

Laurence's voice came through the room. "Ellie. Do you think you could do me a favour?"

A favour? Eleanor wasn't sure what to expect, and it sparked her nerves. "What is it?"

"Go into the corner of the room for me. We're going to be importing your workout equipment. Your body may feel a little funny for a second, as we're calibrating your feedback beyond simple touch and pressure." he said.

"Oh." Ellie sighed. "No problem. Which corner?" she asked.

"Hold on," Then a few seconds later: "Facing away from the screen, the one on the far left."

Eleanor stood up and walked over to the corner, noticing as she did that her movements felt a little slower. The body she had was not as instantaneous to respond, and it took greater care and effort to actually fire her 'muscles', to send the request between brain and body. She stopped at the corner and turned around, and in the opposite corner of the room a series of apparatus appeared in quick succession from the ground up. At first it seemed just a regular armature, a series of steel beams, but it quickly coalesced into a squat rack, a bench and a selection of free weights, along with two or three pieces of cardio equipment. After it had all appeared, a small green light blinked, and Laurence said, "Okay. You can move around again now. We just had to make sure that we weren't going to accidentally put a beam through you, especially now that you're able to feel it."

Ellie peered up sharply toward the corner. "I can feel it?"

"Yes. The only way we could make it so that you would recognise that working out was resistive was to make it cause you discomfort, unfortunately. So now you're able to feel pain again." He paused. "Sorry about that."

Great. *Ellie thought,* because what my mind really needs is accurate pain receptors after my last memory in the real world was a fucking car crash.

* * *

"Three days?" the director asked, motioning to Eleanor's body breathing softly in the bed. She was healing, slowly.

"We think so, yes." the doctor nodded and gestured to a nearby wall display. Eleanor's vitals were buzzing there, along with a set of charts that appeared unusual for doctors' analyses. "We're almost certain that she's recovered from the trauma of the crash, to the point that having consciousness won't cause her any mental trauma. That said, she *will* be sore for months, and some of her wounds will still require monitoring."

"No infections or anything?" the director pressed.

"Not visible at this stage. We had one early on, but we caught it. That large laceration was caused by a piece of rubber and glass that had been hit by other crash debris." The doctor replied. "Now that none of the wounds are open, we're less concerned. The breaks in her legs have healed and shouldn't give her any problems, but the fracture in her ulna may give her limited rotational mobility in her hand."

"And brain function?"

"Well, obviously she hasn't got a *consciousness* to speak of at the moment, so no. However, synaptic pathways seem to be intact from what we can see, and by sending light electrical signals through a neural lace that we place over her head, we can see the places we'd expect to see light up. She has no bleeding into the brain cavity, so that's another positive sign." The doctor checked another page of his notes. "We've been giving her brain regular stimulus every few hours just to make sure the neural pathways stay active, until your people can transfer her back."

The director nodded, then turned and got her phone out, calling a number. Laurence's face appeared on the screen.

"Yeah?" he greeted.

"We need to start running protocols for getting Eleanor back into her body," the director said. "Wheels up in 3 days."

* * *

Two days later, Laurence had finished optimising the subroutines that would allow the conscious simulacrum of Ellie to be ported back into the body of the woman. Loaded into the program at the moment were two small pieces of test data. On their own they represented a nearly infinitesimal amount of brain memory, when compared to the database that was Ellie's brain, but it allowed him to run tests quickly and debug, and when he pulled the chart up it would be small enough to view immediately without having to waste time zooming in and out. Laurence tapped the command to bring up the matching dialog.

A small chart appeared. It generated as a series of blue and yellow bars of different sizes, arranged horizontally. Each blue and yellow bar was set as a pair, with most of the pairs nearly identical in thickness, size and length, with only a few bars having vastly different inputs. To the right of each pair, running down the screen, was a percentage.

Laurence didn't see any red values, which was good, as the synthesized data had been created to represent two pieces of data that differed only slightly from each other. After all, Ellie's mind had been only absent from her physical brain for a few weeks, so opportunity for meaningful change was minimal.

The number at the base shone green, and Laurence smiled. They matched closely enough that it was highly improbable for a consciousness to suffer any real ill effects from the transfer. *Now for the big one,* he thought. He'd taken a copy of Ellie's consciousness as soon as they'd brought it in, and another one only a couple of hours after they'd brought her back up into the simulation. Both of them were useless from a consciousness standpoint now, as they hadn't been maintained as such - he'd essentially just taken a static screenshot of the two moments in time. When they did this for real, it would be taking Ellie's current mental state, and transferring it in real time to her body. Creating a copy wasn't really an option.

Laurence navigated to the location of the two files and loaded them in. The multi-million-dollar machine sagged under the load of the data, and the cooling fans sprang to life.

This would take a while. Laurence went and made a cup of coffee.

* * *

Ellie was deadlifting, musing at the fact that despite the effort she could feel, she didn't sweat. That, and the continued lack of sleep made her appreciate the way that the body healed all the more. The muscle soreness that was felt a couple of days after a hard session was a lot worse for the mind to deal with when you couldn't sleep through the worst of it.

"Hey, Ellie." Laurence's voice echoed from its corner of the room, back again for his daily chat. Ellie appreciated the company. She had been in the simulation for at least eight weeks that she was aware of, and she was keen to get out and thank the man who, to her knowledge, had single-handedly kept her sane during her stay inside the computer.

"Hey Laurence." Ellie smiled, pausing between reps. "How much longer?"

"I'm running some base data now. We'll know in about half an hour whether or not it will work."

Ellie sighed with relief. "Thank *fuck* for that. I've been pacing the room. Cabin fever is super intense when you know that an *outside* doesn't even *exist* in any real sense." *Not that inside does either,* she didn't add.

"You must be aching to get out."

"Absolutely," Ellie huffed, and brought up the image of herself on the screen. There had been several people in the room, monitoring her body constantly for the past few days. They had brought with them computer equipment to start with, and then slowly constructed a separate mesh of fine wires. Ellie wondered idly whether she was being stored in that computer. The mesh was laced with glass tubes that shone like fairy lights, and the whole structure sat on a delicate geodesic-dome-like frame. The construction lasted the better part of a day and night, and once completed, the team carefully lifted it and placed it on Eleanor's head. A different team came in with a large trolley full of measurement equipment and small screwdrivers and other tools. For another six hours, they'd taken measurements of all the nodes of the dome and made adjustments to the distance and size of each of them.

"Why are they doing that?" Ellie asked.

"It's an electromagnetic transmitter." Laurence replied. "We're essentially beaming you back into your own head, and we need to know that you're going back into the right spot. When we got you out it was easier, because we could configure the computer to match what your brain was doing. This time though, we haven't really got a blank slate to play with. We need to get it right to about one ten-thousandth of a millimeter."

"Can you do that?"

"If you stay still," Laurence joked. "But you haven't been the most active customer in the last few weeks so I think we're fine. It just takes time to calibrate."

* * *

The team surrounding her body murmured amongst themselves. One of the scientists produced a tablet, on which he loaded a program. The technician buzzing about Eleanor's head stepped back to inspect the screen, then nodded, giving her thumbs up. The scientist with the tablet nodded in return, and keyed a series of inputs until a three-dimensional, rotating image of the brain appear, with a spreadsheet of numbers next to it. A green indicator appeared in the lower right corner.

"Looks like we're all set!" Laurence said.

Seeing as he had the ability to pull a new brain scan from the real Eleanor, as well as a test case for the simulacrum, Laurence decided to rerun the congruence test with a more up-to-date dataset. The real transfer was going to happen tomorrow, and the more data he had, the more he'd be able to use for the paper he was thinking of putting together. He'd have to wait to get Ellie's permission of course, but they had built a rapport, so he didn't see that being a substantial issue. Sipping his coffee, he sent an instant message to the head of the neural interlace team and requested that she pull a brain image. He paused the simulation he'd been running - the results were in an acceptable range, anyway. A little wider than expected, but acceptable still. The whirring machine settled down to its normal hum. Then he wheeled himself back to the watch desk for Ellie's chamber and started a similar freeze frame to the one he'd done before. Both of them would take a while to complete, but he knew where the files would be when they were done. He pointed a small script at the two of them, telling it to load them both into the brain congruence scan. Tapping his fingers on the desk excitedly, he waited to get confirmation from all the commands he'd just pulled, and then swept out of the office. He'd need a good sleep tonight.

＊＊＊

Laurence's coffee was nearly cold, its surface quivering as he took stock.

He had his hands the same way he'd been holding them since he'd turned the screen back on that morning. One was hanging loosely by his side, the other gripping the coffee. It was this hand that was shaking, the unnoticed strain of slowly choking the handle tighter and tighter as he drank before the screen.

There were more blue and yellow bars this time. The numbers on the side were reduced to single pixels, and the bars themselves were interpolated to the point where not all of them could be seen when the whole graph was in view. The screen was a blue and yellow haze. And the large number down the bottom held a small, glowing red number that had caught Laurence's attention. He'd stood frozen, staring at it whilst what warmth remained in his coffee leached into the otherwise empty room.

"Fuck," he said.

* * *

The director rocked back in her chair, face drawn and dark. "What happened?"

"I don't know yet." Laurence twitched, chin gripped by his pent fingers. "The nearest I can figure is that the introduction to a new environment, and the changes to her consciousness we've been making through the mainframe, have resulted in unusually high neuroplasticity. That's not normal for people past puberty. That, and the regular impulses given by the medical team wouldn't have been directed at any brain area in particular, and could have altered her brain makeup." Laurence said. "Either way, we can't make the transfer."

"Have you told her yet?" The director asked.

"Not yet... I wanted to see you about it first." Laurence said.

And I don't want to tell her, he thought, *because I got too close to her and now delivering bad news is going to hurt even more.*

The director eyed him sharply past her furrowed brow. His thoughts had to be written clearly on his face - Laurence could have kicked himself. *This* is why you maintain a professional distance. The poor woman.

"I'll see if we can workshop a solution of some sort. My hopes aren't high though. You go and tell her what's wrong," she said.

"I will do," he said. *I can be there for her.*

* * *

"Same corner?"

"Yes please." Laurence's voice had a worried edge to it, which Ellie didn't like the sound of. She went obediently and stood in the corner. As before, a strange armature appeared before her and it slowly formed itself into something that made more sense. Her eyes widened as the torso of a humanoid form appeared in the centre, and crude arms, legs and a head appeared shortly after. A fleshy mass congealed to cover the model, and then colour appeared, and a man stood in front of her.

It was Laurence, she knew instantly. And he had a look on his simulated face that made her worried. "What is it?" she said.

"I wanted to be here. I have to tell you this and it seemed like it would be best to do it in person." He shrugged, "Well, as in person as it can be."

"Are you... did you *upload* yourself?" she asked.

"What? Oh, no." he said, "I've built a 3D version of myself on a generic skeleton, and I'm using a VR setup to get myself in here. I'm glad it worked."

Ellie nodded, apprehensive. "So, what's the deal?"

"Well…" he paused, gathering his thoughts. "I'm not sure how to say this, but at this stage… we don't know how to get you back".

Ellie froze. Her mind went blank, and she stared at Laurence. The first quasi-real interaction she'd had with the form of another human being in months. He'd built a version of himself just to tell her *this*.

She started to reel, and her blank confusion gave way to fury. *You mean I'm fucking STUCK in here?* "What do you mean you don't know? What do you MEAN? How the FUCK did you think you were going to get me back? What went wrong?!"

Laurence, trying to hold in the grimace of his guilt, held his hands out to the abuse. "I'm sorry. I'm *so* sorry." He croaked, shrinking into himself. Ellie growled, her only sanity coming from the man's remorse, even if it didn't grant her anything.

"We thought that because adults are less neuroplastic than children, that introducing their cerebral capacity to a new environment would simply mean that they would reform their adult brain 'shape' within the new environment. It would appear that we were wrong."

"It would fucking well appear that way, wouldn't it?" Ellie snarled, acid lining her voice. "What am I supposed to do? Just sit around in this room forever? I've only stopped myself going mad because I thought at least, at LEAST I wouldn't be stuck in here. I've been watching myself…" She pointed her terse, daggered finger at the screen, "…slowly getting better for *days on end* and telling myself that *at least* I wouldn't be stuck inside a fucking computer much longer! And now I'm going to be stuck here because you *assumed* you knew everything? You assumed before you'd even begun, as if my livelihood, my *sanity*, my *happiness* was just some gamble that you owned? For what?"

Ellie hissed, and Laurence had nothing for her but a strange 3D-modelled quiver of the lip. "*Fuck* you."

Laurence tried to form a response. In this strange world, this odd binary place, Ellie could almost *feel* his brain working to compute its solution, but she didn't care. Unless Laurence had a miracle solution right now – which he clearly didn't – Ellie wanted out. She was fuming. She was so *sick* of being stuck in this slightly unreal place, with its blank walls and its stupid equipment and the unending wakefulness and that *dickless* fucking voice. *Laurence's* stupid voice. The one person she'd had contact with for two months, who had been *selfless* enough to preserve her sanity, had neglected to mention that her survival beyond this unending isolation hinged on some outlandish windfall lottery. Ellie was desperate to hit him, to lash out in violent rage and beat him, but a small corner of her mind reminded her that it was no use. He couldn't feel anything in here any more than the bed could, or the wall. Laurence was just a fake projection of himself, in a fake projection of a room, hooked up to a fake projection of her mind.

He looked at her, the slightly-too-glassy eyes marred with regret. "I'm sorry Ellie, but that's not all."

She stared, uncomprehending, already overwhelmed by the helplessness of the situation. "What do you mean, 'that's not all'? What else could there *possibly* be?"

Laurence advanced a small step toward her. "Well, the consciousness that you describe as 'you' currently only exists in one live state, and that's on a super high throughput server at the lab of our company. There are backups that I've kept but they're merely images; inert. They're no more alive or conscious than any other computer file."

"So?" Ellie pushed him. "What does that mean for me? How

is this worse than what you've already told me?"

Laurence sighed, and stepped again, "The server has a limited capacity. And without a clear path of precedence on what to do with a human consciousness that's trapped in a computer, we can't really, well… other projects are likely to require the computing power."

"Other projects?" Ellie hushed. "Can't they just go to another computer, or server, or drive, or *something*?"

Laurence bit his lip, his head shaking to each suggestion. "We don't have the…"

Ellie couldn't believe it. She felt like she'd been punched in the gut. "You're going to switch me off?!"

"Not me. And not now. But eventually the resources will be in demand, or the server will need a reboot, or god forbid there will be a power loss. We can't just…"

It was too much. Ellie crumpled onto the floor. The synaptic response that the environment team had been honing so carefully obeyed silently as her senses overloaded and her mind gave up. She pulled her legs toward her with her arms and cried in great wracking, heaving sobs. Laurence knelt next to her awkwardly, his body slightly wrong in the angles of the knees and elbows as the motion capture suit flexed around him. She rocked backward and forward, pressing her eternally dry eyes against her knees. Laurence put his arms around her, the too-familiar voice cooing in her ear.

"I'm sorry, Ellie. I'm so sorry." Over and over and over again. She could barely hear him, eyes squeezed shut, stuck in that hateful perfect box that she couldn't leave - but she didn't want to *die*. His arms and body pressed against her, cold and unforgiving, a presence no more meaningful than the frosty seat of a bus shelter on a winter's day. She looked at the screen, where two orderlies were taking vital sign readings of the silent woman in the bed.

I've been dead for months, she thought. *I just didn't know it.*

***

The director was running the workshop with a single-minded purpose. She'd gathered the environments team, the medical team, the computer technicians headed up by Laurence, and the people who had developed the neural interlace. All of them had been standing in a loose circle around a series of whiteboards and screens for several hours now, but were no closer to getting Eleanor back into her own head.

The initial thought had been that they may have been able to massage the 'shape' of the thought patterns in the simulation to that of the shape of the real brain they had. They were able to manipulate large swathes of data in the computer, after all. Eleanor's mind was simply another dataset, albeit a highly complex one which needed to be managed carefully so that none of it would be corrupted.

The idea had been discarded as far too risky. A consciousness with no backup is not something to mess with when you aren't sure what the ramifications would be. They were in deep enough at the moment; it would be likely that Eleanor would need extensive counselling when they got her out.

If they got her out.

"Okay. So how bad is it? How much drift has actually occurred?" asked the neural lace engineer.

Laurence was the one to reply. "Enough. She's about five percent below the margin we'd call 'unsafe'. That margin was put in place with the expectation that two times out of three, the patient would *not* receive brain damage. Below that the probability gets exponentially worse."

"Two times out of three? So she's below the threshold where *thirty-three percent of the time*, she's getting some sort of brain malfunction?" the director said.

Laurence's deep sigh, along with the way he stared morosely into the distance, was all the answer she needed.

"Do we know what caused it?"

The Environments team leader chimed in. "Partially, we think it has to do with the amount of tinkering we've done with what amounts to her 'input-output' system. To make her viable as a digital consciousness, we had to change a lot about the way she received information. We simply don't have the knowledge of how the nervous system works with the body to make it work effectively. So, we blocked or modified neural pathways so that the simplified versions of the environments, and bodily work that we completed, were able to be integrated cleanly. As a result, there seems to have been a fundamental shift in her brain patterns."

The head doctor also spoke up. "Additionally, the misdirected firing of small impulses to keep her brain matter intact was unavoidable - but it was unwise. The impulses we used were simple sine wave currents, intended to light as much synaptic pathway up as possible, with no real regard for whether the pathways would change as a result. None of us made the connection that we would be making such a fundamental change to her neural structure. Although in honesty, if we hadn't sent the impulses her brain would likely have rotted. We were doing the best with the information we had." The slump of his shoulders spoke to the defeated feeling of the entire room.

The director nodded. "Noted. So from both ends, there has

been drift from the initial conditions she was brought here with, and now they're irreconcilable. We can't change her patterns now to match as we don't know whether it'll work, and her consciousness might be irreparably damaged. We also can't change the living tissue because we lack the apparat–"

Laurence spoke up. "Wait. We do have the apparatus, don't we?" He looked at the neural lace team. "You're going to be pushing her back into her head using that dome you built, right? That's using electro-magnetic high frequency impulses?" Two of the team members eyed each other curiously, then nodded. Laurence rounded on the medical staff, "And you've got a device to send electrical impulses into the tissue to keep it active?"

The doctor picked up on the suggestion. "Yes! We can connect the two together. By using Eleanor's simulated brain pattern and movements as a guide, we can 'nudge' the living tissue into a state that more closely resembles her consciousness!"

The neural net team was drawing furiously on the board. It was a makeshift transformer to convert the sine wave that had been used for impulses into something that could be used to transmit more complex data. Laurence's team was feeding them numbers about necessary congruence ratios, and the doctors started talking amongst themselves about how much of an impulse could be directed to change the brain stem in one go.

"This will have to be done in stages, we can't switch the whole pattern at once…"

"… going to have to reduce the output of that dynamo, that's not subtle enough…"

"… we'll need to keep it cool, if we overheat the system we'll have to rebuild it…"

"…should perform a congruence test after each impulse to make sure it's getting better."

The director watched, heavy eyes gleaming from behind hair that'd had too many a hand run through it since being carefully put together that morning. The four teams were agitated, jumping with excitement. The problem was nearly solved, and this first-in-the-world case study scenario was looking more and more likely to have a successful solution. The director turned and looked at Laurence, his hair bedraggled and eyes gaunt from lack of sleep. His steps were, however, full of energy, and he bounded toward her.

"Can I tell her?" he asked.

The director nodded.

* * *

The preceding days had been the worst of the time in the box, Ellie had decided. Her horror had given way to incredulity, which had given way in turn to joy, then excitement, then once again settled on impatience. She had watched the teams work through the necessary steps over and over again, as they connected a series of synthesised neural maps to the impulse, then calibrated and fired. After each attempt, they reran the hour-long test of congruence between her mind and her brain. The sight was somehow both boring and riveting. She was watching her own brain take shape in real time.

Laurence was busy with the work, advising the teams on which sections needed the most work. In a way it was like watching a sculptor, but the clay was the human brain. He was meticulous in his detail, and she watched him on the screen for hours as he consulted and consolidated and assisted the others that were there.

At the end of each day, he'd come and check in on her. The

body he'd built to visit her was a comfort, and something nice to have around as she waited to come back into the real world. He usually didn't have much energy left for talking, but the physical presence was something she looked forward to. The entire team looked exhausted, slumping with heavy eyes about their work, but they pushed on and on and on, with eighteen-hour days not uncommon. Ellie felt that her sleeplessness would have helped, if she was somehow there doing the work. She decided at one point that when they got her out, she'd buy each and every one of them a drink. But especially Laurence. He was the one who had been there to help her from the beginning, and who personally told her when he thought it would end, and who came back not two days later to tell her that they could do it. They could bring her back.

Finally, it came. A congruence test came back with all the indicators green. The two minds were now close enough to the same that they knew with 99% certainty that she'd be able to go back with no ill effects. Laurence saw the result come through, the small glowing green symbol, and turned to the camera. His grin was enormous, and he gave her a thumbs-up.

A few hours later, the net had been retrofitted back to its original purpose, and Laurence's voice came through the room for the final time. "You'll probably not feel anything, but in about ten minutes we're going to hit go on this thing. See you on the other side, Ellie."

"Same to you, Laurence." she replied, her smile soft and hopeful.

Ellie perched herself on the bed, and waited, her mind buzzing and her emotions wired. Her wait, for the jittering of her imaginary heart, seemed eternal, but finally a small indicator light came onto the workstation trolley. The neural net technician strolled up, took a note, and hit a command.

Ellie still felt nothing, but she saw a progress bar appear, moving achingly slowly as all the pieces of herself were put back in place, piece by piece by piece. An enormous flood of relief washed over her. It was over. Her wait was over.

As the progress bar filled, she realised how lucky she'd been to have been in this position at all. Though it had been harrowing and terrifying, she had survived being hit at full speed by a bus. Anyone who hadn't been lucky enough to be in her position would have been killed in that moment. A profound feeling of satiety, of knowing that the best had been done for her, made her glow with happiness.

The progress bar was nearly full. Ellie sat down on the couch now, and watched as her final moments in the room ticked away from her. Soon she would be free. The doctors were milling about, and observing as vital signs not seen for months started to jump into more normal activity. One doctor was taking her pulse and watching her breathe.

As the doctor observed her, Ellie opened her eyes.

She watched, smiling as she realised it had worked, that her consciousness had gone back into her true body, and that she–
Wait.

Why was she still in the room?

The woman in the bed was trying to smile, and Laurence was stumbling toward her, his eyes teary. Ellie's mind raced, and she felt the space where her heart should have been thudding like a jackhammer.

They hadn't *moved* her. They'd *copied* her. She was still in the room, *and* out in the real world. The consciousness transfer had worked, but she was still an echo, trapped in the computer's memory.

She had to warn someone.

She *couldn't stay in here.*

Ellie yelled at the room, but there would be nobody to hear her. They'd turned the sound off. She could see one of the environments team walking to the computer, one member reaching for a button. Their finger danced for the standby switch ready to shut the computer down. Ellie gagged, panicked. She *was* going to die after all.

She ran to the wall and tried to hit it, to warn people and let them know. "LET ME OUT!" she screamed. "I'M STILL STUCK IN HERE!"

She slammed her open palm onto the white void, staring at the screen where, until a few moments ago, her real face had been smiling up at the doctor, and at Laurence. Where she'd just watched her consciousness copied and reinstated to its proper place. "SOMETHING HAS GONE WRONG!" She hit the wall again and again and again. *"I'M STUCK IN HERE!"*

She turned and moved to another wall, hopeless as it was. Whether or not they could even see her didn't matter. She had to find a way to *communicate* with the outside of the simulation. Had to tell them that her mind was still present in the computer, and that the real world her was only a carbon copy of the consciousness the team had so carefully built.

She went to slam her hand on the other wall, but it disappeared. Whether it was her hand or the wall itself that disappeared she couldn't say, though in reality she understood that one assumed the other. Her mind, attempting to flail at a surface, was now only a thought pattern, with no physical sensation to back it up. She realised that she couldn't see, or hear, and as she realised it, the meaning of the words slipped from her. Her ability to perceive gave way, and all that was left of the woman named Eleanor was a digital spike of what passed for adrenaline. She was frozen for an eternal, unending moment, as a perfect simulacrum of abject terror.

Preview: Spice Trader

Please enjoy this preview chapter of Spice Trader, *Henry Neilsen's next book, out October 31, 2020.*

I first heard of Spice while I was out at some nightclub or other. I'd have a better memory of exactly where if I hadn't been shitfaced three nights a week for six years. There's a point at which every night becomes a blur of lights and thumping bass tones. The cloying press of bodies sweating out the myriad toxins they'd drunk, snorted, smoked or otherwise imbibed didn't change. The faces of the hookups vanished with the hangovers the next day. I couldn't rightly remember where exactly it was, I just knew I'd had enough of paying too much for watered down drinks and I needed a hit.

One of the guys I was out with gave me 'the look' from across the room, and I knew he had something. I extricated myself from the girl I was dancing with and walked towards him. I'd already dropped a bunch of pills; it probably looked like I was having an epileptic fit in forward motion, but it felt smooth at the time. The place had an outdoor smoking area where you could sneak a joint if you were careful, or chat up whoever you'd been dancing with. I pulled out a cigarette and dangled it loosely from my mouth as I stumbled through the press of bodies, feeling for the zippo in my jeans. The security guard at the back door eyed me as I tried to walk past nonchalantly. I pulled out the lighter and flicked it a few times as I walked toward my friends. They were standing up; the seating had been taken long ago by the chain-smokers. It was that kind of a place. They were standing underneath a worn umbrella that bore the label of some middle-market beer.

Jemima rolled her eyes, and I jerked back as she made an attempt to take the cigarette out of my mouth. "Christ, Pete, when are you gonna give that up? Gives you cancer, yeah?"

"Fuck off," I said. I thought it was a bit hypocritical of her; she was no stranger to party drugs after all. Smoking seemed to genuinely disgust her, though. "You got some stuff or what? I was on with that chick in there so you've got to make it up to me." I pretended to thrust my hips at her.

Jem laughed. "In your dreams. You came of your own free will, any nookie you've missed out on is your own fault." She held up her hands, an indication of innocence, thin fingers outstretched. "As it so happens, Pat's given me a treat. Something new." With that, she reached down her top and plucked out a small baggy full of white powder.

"You know I haven't got enough for fucking coke," I said.

Patrick sat up at this. He'd been watching our conversation with dilated pupils, slumped back against the fence. He was blasted in that particular way you can only get when you really work at it, and Pat made a point of keeping a small pharmacy running through his bloodstream. Drugs, for him, were more professional than recreational.

"'S called 'Spice,'" he slurred, staggering over, "and it's fucking great."

"Has he had any?" I asked with a sideways look to Jem, "'cause if it fucks me that much, I'm out."

Jemima glanced at Patrick. "He has, but that's not his problem. He's off his brain on Horse at the moment."

Pat was staring at the space in between us. Jem had the baggy proffered to me still. I snatched it from her and snuck it into my jeans before anyone could see what we were doing.

"What's it like? It's not some shit like Krokodil or anything completely evil, right?" I'd seen enough images of the melting skin of Krokodil users to be wary of any new drug on the market. A high wasn't worth losing your teeth, eyes or skin over. I didn't fancy getting lesions or any of the other nasties you got with Krokodil either.

"It's nothing like that! It's good, trust me." Pat had come back to life after I'd slipped the baggy into my pocket. The sidelong glance I gave Jem transmitted my thoughts to her. *Can I trust this?* I asked her silently.

"It's not just chalk wrapped in noodle dust. It's good. Have a go."

I nodded, downed my beer, slipped my finger into my jeans to make sure the baggy was still there, and turned to the bathroom. I'd like to think I'd have been a little more difficult to convince, but I trusted Jem. Pat was trashed, but he didn't seem likely to fall into a seizure or start clawing at his face any time soon.

You can tell when an establishment caters for drug addicts and miscreants as soon as you go to the bathroom. This place knew exactly what people were there for. I heard a rhythmic thud coming from the fully enclosed cubicle next door, along with muffled moans to match. I locked the door behind me and pulled the baggy and my wallet from my jeans. The graffiti on the walls leered down at me, juxtaposing the once-polished concrete floor, damp with the badly aimed urine of a thousand patrons. The place was filthy. Despite this, people in here had been careful to ensure the stainless-steel sink was dry, wiped down, and devoid of any of the nastiness in the rest of the room.

I did my part, wiping down the side of the basin with a piece of paper towel from the dispenser. Next, a fifty-dollar bill and a credit card from my wallet. I pulled them out, and held them in two fingers with the baggy as I returned the wallet to my jeans. I poured an appropriate-looking amount of the powder onto the flat side of the basin. A distorted reflection stared hungrily back at me. Working with careful precision I cut the pile into a line with the credit card. It had a slightly different feel to it than some of the other drugs I'd tried. It was more crystalline but somehow softer, and almost seemed to glimmer at me in the LED light of the bathroom. *Pearlescent,* I'd have called it if I had been able to think straight.

I stretched, rolling my shoulders back, standing as I rolled the fifty. Once that was done, I hunkered over the sink, pushing one end of the rolled-up note to my nose. I sniffed and moved my head along the line in a movement just short of a jerk.

As I walked back out, the taste still strong in the back of my throat, I felt it hit me.

About the Author

Henry Neilsen hails from Melbourne, Australia. After working as a sound technician, a factory worker, an oyster farmer and myriad other odd jobs, he went to university and studied architecture. He found out that he was rubbish at architecture and now works as a consultant in an engineering firm. When he isn't writing, he is a keen competitive rower who has competed at the Australian national championships. He writes speculative and science fiction, or at the very least stories with a speculative bent to them. He lives with his fiancee Anna and their two cats, Penelope and Ser Pounce.

You can connect with me on:
- http://www.huntingsunrise.com
- https://twitter.com/HuntingSunrise
- https://www.instagram.com/hunting_sunrise

Subscribe to my newsletter:
- http://www.huntingsunrise.com/mailing-list

Also by Henry Neilsen

Spice Trader
Peter, along with his friends Jemima and Patrick, are long time partygoers and recreational drug users. During one of their regular nights out, Patrick introduces the trio to "Spice", a new drug with some special properties. To their knowledge, it has no negative effects, isn't addictive, and can't be traced in the bloodstream.

Several new laws are being proposed. Chief among them are rights of the police to harvest cell phone metadata, and the planned obscelescence of cash-based transactions. Can the three friends keep exploring this exciting new party drug? Or will the powers that be come down on when their data starts unravelling their story?

Eleanor wakes up alone, in a near-featureless room with no windows or doors. A voice speaks to her from an unseen source: she's been in a car accident, and her mind has been transferred to a computer for safekeeping.

It's the first time the medical team has tried this.

Can they keep her mind sane long enough to heal her body, and if so, can they reunite them?

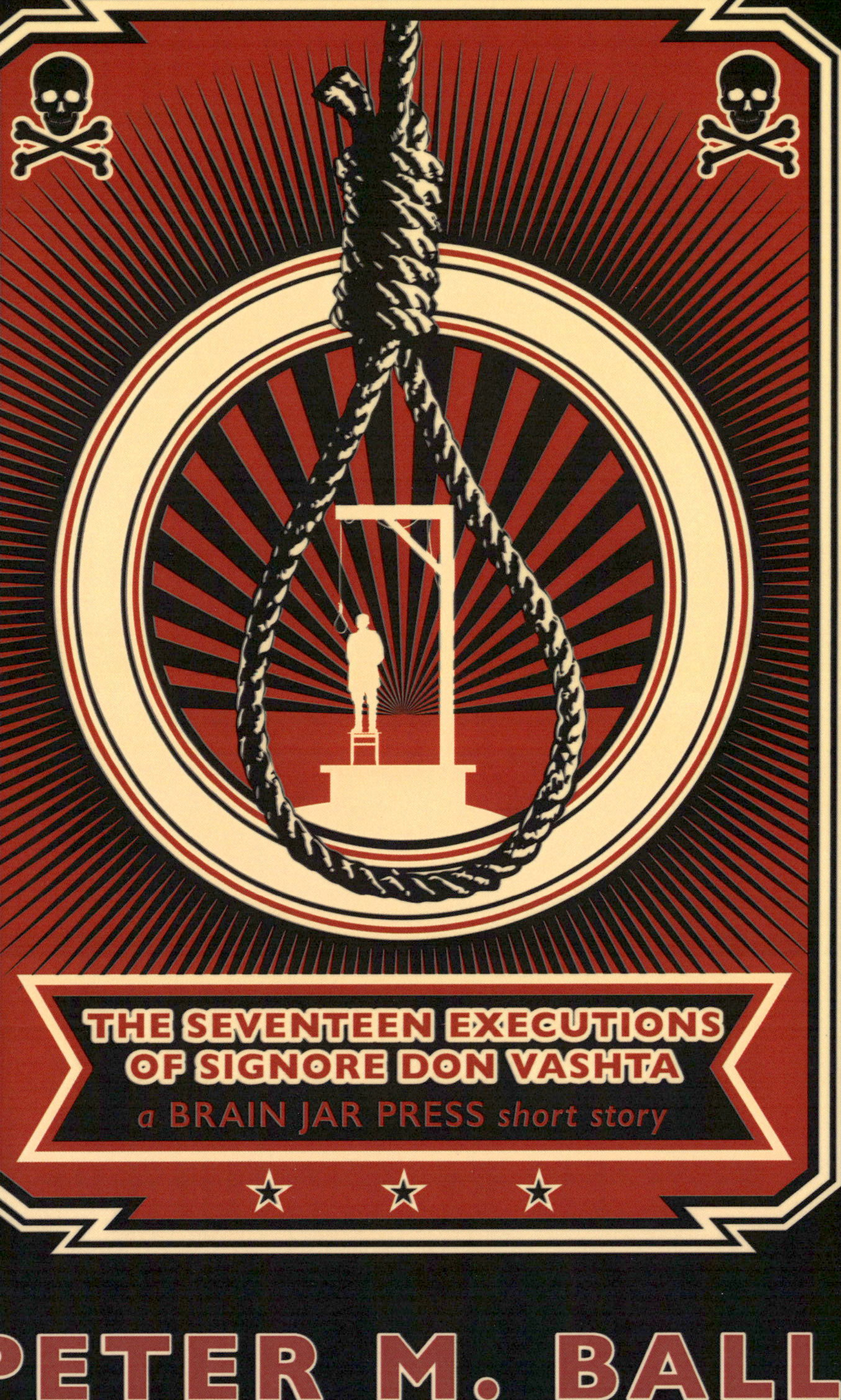

THE SEVENTEEN EXECUTIONS
OF SIGNORE DON VASHTA
a BRAIN JAR PRESS short story
PETER M. BALL